ONE too many) LIES

L. A. BOWEN

An imprint of Enslow Publishing

WEST 44 BOOKS™

Please visit our website, www.west44books.com. For a free color catalog of all our high-quality books, call toll free 1-800-542-2595 or fax 1-877-542-2596.

Cataloging-in-Publication Data

Names: Bowen, L.A.
Title: One too many lies / L.A. Bowen.
Description: New York : West 44, 2019. | Series: West 44 YA verse
Identifiers: ISBN 9781538382493 (pbk.) | ISBN 9781538382509 (library bound) | ISBN 9781538383254 (ebook)
Subjects: LCSH: Children's poetry, American. | Children's poetry, English. | English poetry.
Classification: LCC PS586.3 O548 2019 | DDC 811'.60809282--dc23

First Edition

Published in 2019 by
Enslow Publishing LLC
101 West 23rd Street, Suite #240
New York, NY 10011

Editor: Caitie McAneney
Designer: Sam DeMartin

Photo Credits: cover image Mohd Murtadha Mohamed/EyeEm/Getty Images; back cover (skid marks) wawritto/Shutterstock.com.

Printed in the United States of America

CPSIA compliance information: Batch #CS18W44: For further information contact Enslow Publishing LLC, New York, New York at 1-800-542-2595.

For the women who made me—
Sally, Elsa, Rosemary

I'D RATHER BE OUTSIDE

soaking up the sunshine.

I could be riding my bike
to get some ice cream.
Or even floating
in a friend's swimming pool.

But my bedroom got
a little bit messy
over the summer.

Under piles of
unfolded laundry,
dog-eared notebooks,
and loose papers,
I find a few
useful things.

Like some library books
that are due...yesterday!

And my favorite photo
that I've been using
as a bookmark.

I pin it to the wall
above my bed.

It's a selfie
taken at arm's length.

Up close,
three smiling faces.

Kate, Abby, and I.

Best friends
forever.

(I hope.)

THE PHOTO

Myself in the middle.
All glasses
and long brown hair.

Kate on my right.
With bright blue eyes
and perfect makeup, as usual.

Abby to my left.
Her blonde hair, always changing,
had a pink streak that week.

The photo is cropped close
to hide the background.
What can't be seen,
a party...

Kate's Sweet 16!

I lied when my parents asked
if there was alcohol.

I wasn't the one drinking it.
Honest!

Either way
Mom and Dad
would not
approve.

#BFFS

I remember when we first met
in the sixth grade.
Sitting in the back
of English class.

We loved writing poems.
But mostly we just wrote
secret messages.

Carefully folding
our lined notebook paper
into small triangles.
Which we passed

                                        back

                        and

        forth

whenever
Ms. G.
was looking

                the
                        other
                                way.

FIVE YEARS LATER

we're still making poetry.

Every time we laugh together
it's like free verse.
Without any rules.

We don't always need a reason.
It just comes naturally
when we're together.

When we laugh
our shoulders shake

                                    up

                    and

     down.

But when we cry
it's like we shake

      down

                  and

                                    up

instead.

All backwards
from how it's
supposed to be.

SEPTEMBER

I can't believe it's

    junior year.

Have to think about

    SATs,

    prom,

    and college

this year.

And my parents have made

it clear.

They expect me to earn

    a scholarship

    or two...

to help pay for college.

    We can't afford it

    otherwise.

I've always gotten

pretty good grades.

    Mostly As,

    a few Bs,

    maybe a C

    or two...

but junior year is huge.

It's a lot of work.

    But a chance to really shine.

So I know I have to put in

some extra effort

this year.

Glad it's only

    September.

CAREERS?!

My adviser says
we're supposed to be
thinking about
a career.

Already?

I don't know
what I want to
do
or
be.

I just want to
read
and
write.

Maybe I can be a
journalist,
English teacher,
librarian,
or editor...

maybe an
author,
too.

I HAVE A LOT TO SAY

I love to write
in verse.

The words just
come to me
this way.

Whenever
I sit down
with a pen.

They put one of them
in the school yearbook
last year.

One of my poems.

Which was a little
embarrassing,
actually.

My English teacher,
Mr. Bates,
said,
This is great stuff.

He says this
to everyone.

(Adults lie, too.)

TOP SECRET

I write in my journal
nearly every single day.

Have to keep it hidden
from my little brother
Logan.

He's nine years old.
And he can be
so nosy.

My parents tell him
to stay out of my room
unless he has
permission.

But he snoops anyway.

When Kate
and Abby and I
are hanging out,

we keep my door closed
and we still
have to whisper.

We've got
important things
to talk about.

SHHH!

We talk about anything
and everything.

Like how Kate
stole a pair of jeans at the mall.

(I don't tell her,
but I think it's
a stupid risk to take.)

And how Abby
bought a fake ID from a friend.

(I don't tell her,
but I think she's
out of her mind.)

And how I've
always liked...
Alex Parish.

And I mean really,
really liked.
Forever.

At least, ever since
the sixth grade.

I'm basically
in love with him.

(They don't tell me,
but I know they think
he's a nerd.)

But I actually think
he's really cool.
In a way.

He's funny.
And nice.
And super cute.

Grey-green eyes
under a mop of
straight black hair.

He's on the soccer team
with Kate's boyfriend, Trevor.

But he never
hangs out with us.

He mostly hangs out
with the band kids.

Maybe he's just
not interested...

OCTOBER

Kate and I walk together
most days.

Unless she catches a super-early
ride with her dad.

Sometimes Abby meets us
along the way.

But she's usually
running late.

Out of breath and
puffing on a cigarette.

We talk nonstop
the whole time.

We never run out
of things to say.

Some days I walk alone
but I don't mind.

This time of year
there's so much to think about.

I breathe deeply.
Fresh autumn air.

I try to memorize the way
it all looks and feels.

Green, yellow, orange, red.
And every color in between.

I keep to the edge
of the sidewalk.

Where there's extra leaves
to shuffle through.

And take one last breath
and one last look around.

Before I let the school door
slam behind me.

PHYS. ED.

First period
of the day.
It's too early
for gym class.

My hair is still
wet
from this morning's
shower.

Changing out of jeans
and a new T-shirt
to pull on shorts
and an old T-shirt.

Everybody talks
with their head down
for privacy.

Kate and I linger
in the locker room
tying our shoelaces.

But I guess Abby
skipped today.

Not a
big surprise.

WE NEED A PARACHUTE

I miss gym class like
when we were kids.

Freeze tag. Kickball.
Red light, green light.
And days spent
on the playground.

But my favorite
was the giant parachute
that came out once
or twice a year.

Each kid held the edge
and lifted it up high
over their head.
Then real quick,
they all ducked below.

Everyone underneath
in the colorful glow
of the parachute.

Twenty or so kids
grinning ear to ear
for a brief second
before the sheet
fell down
over us
again.

WE NEED OXYGEN

Now it's
volleyball,
basketball,
    and sometimes
    swimming.

I hate swim days.

Today we do
    the mile run.

Four laps
    around the track.

I'm not the fastest,
    but I'm not the slowest.

We run around
    and around
    and around
    and around—one last time.

With each step
we shake
        up   down.
              and

Kate is faster
but would rather
run by my side

talking about
    whatever.

I'm breathing too hard
    to talk.

Sometimes I say,
    uh-huh.

I know we're supposed to
    breathe through our nose.

But I always breathe
    through my mouth.

    uh-huh
    uh-huh
    uh-huh

Gasping
        down   up.
           and

I imagine my
lungs and heart
pumping oxygen
to my muscles.

A fragile,
strong machine.

For this reason
I will never try
one of Abby's
cigarettes.

ENGLISH

Kate and I are in
the same English class,
too.

We don't pass notes
the way we did
when we were kids.

But we sometimes
pass looks
from across the room.

It's like we know exactly
what the other
is thinking.

One glance—
our eyes
say it all.

It's the little things
that get us through
the day.

Don't get me wrong—
we're *kind* of
nerds.

I mean
we're in advanced English
after all.

And it's my
favorite class.
Most days.

Mr. Bates
is actually
a pretty cool
teacher.

But it's
our last class
of the day.

And today
is Friday.

T. C . I . F.

This week really
d r a g g e d
by.

Sometimes I wonder
what it would be like
to skip school with Abby.

But
            I never would.

I don't want to ruin my
perfect record.

But it's like I'm so done
with this place.

Ready for the next
big thing.

But also not ready
for college...

I don't want to be an adult
yet.

But I don't want to be treated like a kid
anymore.

I just want to have more

                    fun.

I just want to have more

                    freedom.

SLEEPOVER AT MY HOUSE

Kate spends the night
at my house.

Abby never texted us back.
So who knows where she is.

We work on homework
for a couple of hours.
Then watch a movie
in the living room.

Mom makes us popcorn,
but she skimps
on the butter.
A healthy snack.

Now don't stay up too late!
she says, when she goes to bed.

Okay Mom...
we'll head up in a few,

I lie.

But I know we're
just getting started.

Because lately the fun doesn't begin
until the parents
leave.

Let's have some more
of that wine!
Kate says.

Last time Abby was here,
she made us try some.

We didn't really enjoy it.
But we all pretended to.

Okay, just a little,

I agree.

I don't know why
Kate wants to drink
this stuff again.

I hate the bitter taste.

But we both laugh
when we see that
it stains our lips
red.

MY FIRST F

Sitting in the back
of class.

I'm too far away to hear
anything.

I'm too far away to see
the board.

I'm not even sure
what the subject is.

A teacher
I don't recognize
hands back a test
I don't remember taking.

And there's a giant

in red.

It seems that
I'm really in
over my head.

How did I let
things slide
like this?

It's not a good
start to the year.
That's for sure.

I wake up sweating.
Frustrated with myself.
Until I realize
it was just a dream.

I've never gotten an **F**
and I don't plan to.

TYPICAL MORNING

Kate and I meet at Abby's locker,
not sure if she'll show.

Finally a familiar streak of blonde hair
rounds the corner.

Where were you on Friday?
I ask.

What was Friday?
Abby asks.

Uh, school!

Did I miss anything fun?
Abby asks.

Not really. We had to do the mile run...

Then I'm glad I wasn't there,
Abby says.

Aren't you worried about your grades?
I ask.

You know the answer to that question...
Abby laughs.

Also, we had a sleepover,
I say.

I just didn't feel like it,
Abby says.

This hurts a little.

But Kate and I pretend
not to care.

I'm kind of glad
when the bell rings.

Abby slams her locker
and we head in

three

separate

directions.

STUDY HALL

Study hall is a good time
to get ahead on homework
and just relax.

Mrs. Randall even lets us
listen to music
with headphones on.

Sometimes I
write in my
journal.

I record any dreams
from the night
before.

Today I finished
the book we're reading
in English class.

It's
Siddhartha
by Hermann Hesse.

We're not
supposed to
jump ahead.

I liked it so much
I just couldn't
stop myself.

I bought my own
faded copy
at a used bookstore.

Underlined all my
favorite parts
in pen.

Now I wish
I hadn't
done that.

I want to be able
to read it
again.

As if
for the very
first time.

LUNCH

I always bring mine.
Sandwich and fruit
in a brown paper bag.

Kate has a big salad.
No dressing,
as usual.

Abby always buys.
She's short
again.

Digging
for
change
in
the
bottom
of
her
purse.

Kate lends Abby
another dollar.

Not that she's
even counting.

HATCHING PLANS

So, are you both
coming over
this Friday?
Kate asks.

I say,
Definitely!

Abby responds
with,
I don't know, maybe.
I might have
other plans...

She trails off.

I wonder
what can be more fun
than a sleepover
with your best friends.

FAMILY DINNER

Friday after school,
I pack an overnight bag.
Pajamas and a toothbrush.

I'm in a hurry
to get to Kate's house.

But Mom and Dad
insist that I stay
to eat dinner
with the family.

Mom makes
homemade pizza,
which is one of
my favorites.

And it's the only
night of the week
when we have soda
at the dinner table.

Though Mom and Dad
each have a glass
of red wine
instead.

They don't notice
there's some missing
from the bottle.

Logan pours
too much dressing
on his salad
because he likes it that way.

He picks all the veggies
off his pizza
and gives them
to me.

Mom and Dad
ask me about school
and stuff.

Are you sure Kate's parents
don't mind you going tonight?
You girls have
so many sleepovers.

I fail to mention
that Kate's parents
aren't even
home tonight.

JUST ANOTHER SLEEPOVER

Kate's parents are out of town,
visiting her brother at college.

And Abby decided to show up
after all.

The perfect opportunity
to stay up late.

Talking about
everything.

We are expert keepers
of secrets.

Whispering out of habit,
though no one is around
to hear us.

No parents.
No siblings.
Just us girls.

We turn on the TV,
open bags of chips and cookies,
and pour big glasses of pop.

I've got an idea,
Kate says.

She finds a bottle of rum
in the kitchen cupboard.
And pours some of the dark liquor
into each glass.

They gulp theirs down.

I take a sip
and cringe at the taste.

Soon they're laughing
and smoking cigarettes.

*Won't your mom smell the smoke
when she gets home?*
I ask.

You worry too much,
Kate says.

LATER, IN THE KITCHEN

I
pour
the
rest
of
my
drink
down
the
drain.

What are you doing in there?
Abby asks
from the other room.

Just getting a glass of water,
I lie.

Abby and Kate are laughing
and rolling around on the living room floor.

They have both spilled some of their drink
on the white carpet.

Do you feel anything yet?
They want to know.

Yeah, I'm really drunk.
Another fib.

I stretch out on the floor
beside them.

I only have to force a smile for a moment,
before I forget that I wasn't having fun.

We stare up at the ceiling
and talk about
boys.

I guess I do feel it
a little bit.

YOU SHOULD TEXT HIM

Abby says.

I don't know,
Kate says.

Invite him over!
Abby demands.
Tell him to bring some guys
        from the soccer team!

My mom would flip
        if she found out!
Kate shrieks.

She picks up her phone anyway
and begins to type with one finger.

The screen is glowing
too bright
in the dark living room.

I put an arm
over my eyes.

I wonder
which friends
Trevor will bring...

TWENTY MINUTES LATER

a car pulls into the driveway.
Going a little too fast.

And parks
half on the front lawn.
Leaving tire marks
in the grass.

(That we will deny
knowing anything about,
when Kate's parents come home
tomorrow afternoon.)

There's a knock
on the door.

When we open it,
there stands Trevor,
and two other guys from school.
Nick and Marcus.

DISAPPOINTED

It's not who I
was hoping for.
Alex.

And nobody is watching
the movie we put on.

Cracking open a beer, I ask,
Where did you guys get these, anyway?

They only laugh
at my question.

I take the smallest
of sips.

A MESS

Soon there are empty cans
everywhere.

Leaving pale rings
on the coffee table.

(That her mom will yell at us for
tomorrow afternoon.)

Kate sits on Trevor's lap
on the couch.

Abby and Nick are alone
in the kitchen.

I pretend to watch
the movie.

Come on. Let's get out of here,
Marcus says,
pointing upstairs.

I follow him.

Only
so that I don't have to stay
here.

I LET HIM KISS ME

Maybe because
I'm bored.

But mostly because
it's easier
than telling him
I'm not interested.

Though even I'm
not sure
if I want to
or not.

He's not
bad looking.

But I hate
every second.

It feels like he's eating
my soul.

I wonder if he even knows
my name.

But I don't have the nerve to ask.

And I will never tell him
that he was my first
kiss.

ENOUCH

I think

as he puts his hands
on my body.

I drank too much,
I lie.

I think I'm getting sick,
I lie.

He sees right through me.

Why is this charade
so much easier
than just saying
NO?

I lock myself inside the bathroom
at the end of the hall.

And I stay there
for an hour
or so.

Looking at my neck
in the mirror above the sink.

Small purple marks.

(That I will spend the next week
hiding from my parents.)

I do feel sick
in a way.

The more I think about
it.

RUMORS

Later I hear
the lies
that Marcus
told his friends.

*We did NOT
do THAT,*

I insist.

I try to laugh it
                    off.

But it really boils
my blood.

IT'S NOT THAT I DON'T WANT TO

It's just that
I don't want to
with you.

Or you.

Or you.

Or you.

Or you.

Or you.

Or you.

Or you.

Or you.

Or you.

Or you.

Or you.

Or you.

SHOW OF HANDS

Mr. Bates asks the class
for a show of hands.

Would any of you be interested
in joining a writing club
after school?

He and another teacher,
Ms. Smith,
are thinking about
starting one.

A few people
shoot their hands
up into the air.

It sounds cool but
I wait a few seconds
before raising mine.

(Only as high
as my shoulder,
with my elbow
still on my desk.)

Kate makes a face
and mouths,
Really?

I shrug.

I know Kate and Abby
think clubs are
super lame.

They'd rather be out
with friends
and boys.

The truth is
I'm not even sure
what writing club
would be like.

Would I have
to read my poems
out loud?

In front of
other people?

I'm scared just
thinking about it.

And I'm already wishing
I had never raised
my hand.

Mr. Bates
looks around,
counting and
smiling.

Well, this is excellent!
he says.

A NEW CRUSH

Alex isn't in any of
my classes this year.
So I never see him.

Except sometimes
in the hallways.

He's always in a rush
to get to class
on time.

But every once in a while
someone new catches
my eye.

Like Peter Marsh
from math class.

Who do you like?
Kate wants to know.

Nobody,
I lie.

HOUSE PARTY

There must be close to
100 people
in Trevor's house.

The party
has just started
and the place is
already a mess.

I fill a cup
with something
that looks like
fruit punch
and tastes like
medicine.

Trying to figure out
how I'm going
to work up the guts
to talk to
Peter.

That's when Kate
grabs my shoulder.

*You've got to come play
spin the bottle!*

I laugh.
No way!
Who even plays
that game anymore?

Peter is playing...
she teases.

Kate! Shhhh!
I know I'm blushing.

How does she always
know these things?

SPIN THE BOTTLE

The odds seem in my favor.
So many cute guys here.
It's just a kiss.

But it doesn't feel that way
when Abby spins
and the bottle points
straight at Peter.

Well that didn't take long.

My stomach turns
as she takes him by the hand
and leads him upstairs.

That's not even how
this game is played!

So there goes my new crush
with one of my best friends.

I feel sick.

I look around the circle.
Is it too late to back out of this?

The group gets
smaller and smaller
as my classmates spin
and pair off.

Suddenly,
it's my turn.
I look around.

Only a few
guys left.

And I realize that I do not want
to kiss any of them.

I close my eyes
and spin anyway.

Please be Marcus.

Something
I never thought I'd wish for.

When I look
the bottle is pointing
straight at *Jamie*.

He's basically
the biggest jerk I know.

He smiles
and licks his lips.

Why did I do this
to myself?

I down the rest
of my mystery punch.

I guess I just
have to get it
over with.

JUST ONCE

On the way to school
Kate and Abby are laughing
at my bad luck.

Jamie is the worst!
they scream.

I know!
I say, shuddering.

He stole my lunch
back in sixth grade,
Abby says.

He gave me a black eye
back in third grade,
Kate says.

You're a traitor!
Abby jokes.

Well, whose idea was it?
I gently shove Kate.

I'm glad she doesn't tell Abby
that I like Peter.

Abby has already bragged
about what happened
upstairs at the party.

56

(And suddenly,
I'm not so interested in him
anymore.)

She doesn't even like him,
but you wouldn't know it.

Abby casually pulls out a joint,
lights it, and starts smoking.

*Trevor hooked us up
with some good green!*

Since when
is this a thing?

Abby laughs
and passes it to Kate.

Then it's my turn.

It smells gross, but
maybe I should try it
         just once.

I'd feel strangely
         left out
otherwise.

I take one
tiny puff...

...and cough
the rest of the way
to school.

PROUD POETS

Kate is my partner for an
English assignment.

So we go to her house
after school.

We have to write
a few poems.

But we're having
writer's block.

*This would be more fun
if we were drunk,*
Kate says.

She pulls out a shoebox
with a few of her dad's beers
which she hid
under the bed.

They are warm and terrible.

We blast music
and let the beer flow
until the words flow.

These are amazing poems!
we agree.

THE NEXT DAY IN CLASS

we read our poems
      out loud.

And suddenly
I realize
they're not
      as good as we thought.

Nobody seems
      to notice.

But I know
I could do
      so much better.

Maybe alcohol
and homework
      don't mix.

SLEEPOVERS AT ABBY'S HOUSE

Her mom's apartment,
or her dad's.

Her mom works
night shifts
at the hospital.

Her dad spends
all night
at the bar.

Either way, they're never home.
And we have the whole place
to ourselves.

Her mom doesn't drink
or keep alcohol
in her house.

And her father has drunk
every last drop
from his liquor cabinet.

But these days,
we don't stick around
for long, anyway. I'm fine with
staying in
and watching a movie.
But Kate and Abby
insist on going out

every time.

Because nobody
is going to notice
when we leave.

And there's always
a party
happening somewhere.

TAXI

Abby buys
a pack of cigarettes
with her fake ID.

While we wait for the cab
in the corner store
parking lot.

It's midnight.

And it's cold enough
that we can see our breath.

But we're not
wearing jackets.
Less to carry.

The female driver
eyes us
but doesn't ask
questions.

I always sit
in the middle.

Kate gives
the address.

And Abby is the first
to strike up a friendly

conversation
with the driver.

Fifteen minutes later
we arrive at a house
in the city.

We split the fare
three ways.
Plus a tip.

The driver says,
You girls
be safe tonight!

And we wear
big smiles
for show.

Thank you!
We always are!

We lie
through our
teeth.

Though we know
she isn't buying it.

AT THE PARTY

We've been looking forward to this
    all week.

There are two kegs on ice
    in the bathtub.

Everyone holds a plastic cup
    full of foam.

I walk up and down the hallways
    of an unfamiliar place.

    Back
            and
                     forth
            and
    forth
            and
                    back.

From room
        to room
                to room.

It feels like I'm moving
    at double speed.

Which is something
    I'm starting to enjoy.

I can't decide in which part of this long house
        the most fun is happening.

Or where the best conversations,
        or the cutest guys, are.

And I like the way it feels,

                just floating

                        in this in-between

        space

        never having to

                        decide

        on one thing

                        or another.

                And maybe not having

                                the ability to.

I SNAP

into focus.
when I hear
people shouting.

I follow
the voices
and push through
the crowd.

And find Kate
lying on the floor.

BLACKOUT

We think about calling
911.

But we don't.

Because maybe
if we wait just a little longer
she will sober up.

And then nobody has to
get in trouble.

Abby sticks her finger
all
the
way
down
Kate's
throat.

Until Kate pukes
                    on the bathroom floor.

There you go.
Get it all out!

I gag
from the smell of it.
Trying not to add to the mess.

I'm beginning to feel
a little sick, myself.

We roll Kate
onto her side
on the cold tile.

*Now we can let her
sleep it off.*

She'll be fine.

*As long as she doesn't
choke
on her own
vomit.*

*Just make sure
she keeps breathing.*

Everyone pretends to know
what's best.
From what we learned in health class
that one time.

But deep down we know
that we know
nothing.

She seems okay now,
we agree.

Obviously.

But…

I stay up
all night.

Watching her chest

                           rise
              and
    fall

with each breath.

      Just in case.

I know she would do the same for me.

      Wouldn't she?

Because that's what
best friends
are for.

Rise

and

fall

and

fall

and

rise.

Is she crying?
Or is she laughing?

Rise

and

fall

and

fall

and

fall

and

fall

and…

Soon, I am also asleep
on the bathroom floor.

HANGOVERS

In the morning,
they act like
nothing happened.

Except that we
all feel
sick.

My head is pounding
and my whole body
aches.

Kate doesn't know
how bad
it got.

She laughs
when we tell her
the details.

I know
one thing
for sure.

I'm never
going to let myself
get that drunk.

CRAMMING

We have so much homework
this year.

Way too much reading to do
for English class.

And so many tests
to study for.

It feels like I'm choosing
between schoolwork
and my social life
every single day.

But I can't seem
to pick just one.

So I struggle
to juggle
both.

Most of the homework
I can finish in
study hall
or lunch
or between classes
or even
during classes,
if I'm honest.

But I can't skip
a single
party.

Things are changing
fast.

I'm afraid of missing
anything.

Because I
feel a
        shift.

And sometimes I worry
that Kate and Abby

                    will
                            slowly
                                        drift
                                                away.

It's a lot of work keeping up
with those two.

And keeping up with
schoolwork, too.

But I'm getting
pretty good at
cramming.

#CANWEGOHOMENOW

Abby met some guy
online.

The second I meet him
I can tell
he's going to be
trouble.

He's older.
How old?
We never ask.

We go to his
apartment.

He offers us white powder
on a tiny spoon.

I say,
No thanks.

But Abby snorts it
up her nose,
eagerly
and expertly.

In the morning
I don't ask too many questions,
but I wonder.

What happened
behind closed doors
last night?

I don't even have to pry.

Abby offers up the story
in great detail
over bagels and coffee.

I can't help admiring her
reckless spirit
in spite of myself.

TWO WEEKS LATER

We walk to the corner store
and wait for Abby
                    outside.

It's her third time buying one
            this year.

She's more afraid of
the disapproving cashier
than of
            derailing her future.

She comes out blushing and
holding a plastic bag,
which she
jams
deep
into
her
purse.

A last ditch effort to   avoid
            all of this.

Are you sure you're ready to find out?
we ask, once we get to her house.

I'm ready,
Abby lies.

She closes the bathroom door
behind herself.

Kate and I sit on the floor
in the hallway.

We exchange nervous glances
that we'd never let Abby see.

Then all three of us
sit on the edge of the tub
holding hands,
waiting.

No one can speak.

Finally.

A single
red line.

A sigh
of relief.

We knew you weren't pregnant!
we lie.

WHEN I GET HOME

Mom is waiting for me
in the kitchen.

Paige, come here!
she calls.

What happened?
I ask.

My heart
is racing.

She knows
something.

You told me
you were staying over
at Kate's house
on Saturday...

she says.

But I saw
Mrs. Knox
at the grocery store
today...

She knows.

Oh, we ended up staying
at Abby's house instead...

I interrupt
as casually
as possible.

...I thought I told you.
Change of plans.

Mom is relieved.

Well, make sure
you let me know
next time.

Sorry, Mom!

I give her a hug
and run upstairs
to fill Kate in
on the new
version of
our story.

ROAD TEST

Kate passes
her road test.

On her third try.
But still.

She even bought a used car
with all the money she saved
from her summer job
at the grocery store.

Now we can go
anywhere.

The world is our
oyster.

And we are
                lost
                        at
                                sea.

125 CRESCENT DRIVE

A couple guys
are smoking on the porch.
They nod and say,
Beer's in the fridge.
Help yourself.

The front door has been left
wide   open.

Because despite the cold,
it's hot inside.

House packed
with bodies.

There's one guy hanging from
a light fixture.

And another guy passed out
on the couch.

So, the usual.

COLLEGE PARTIES

We don't know anyone,
except Eric.

Who shows up
moments later
with a crew of people
and more beer.

This is
his
apartment.

Kate met him
at summer camp
when they were kids.

He's a couple years older.
And so are
all of his friends.

Whenever anyone asks
how old we are
we lie,

Eighteen.

CIRLS DRINK FOR FREE

they say.

But I always chip in,
more than my fair share.

I'm not going to let myself
owe them
anything.

ERIC'S ROOMMATE

When he walks in,
our eyes meet.

Instant connection.

Later, I hear his name
for the first time.

Morgan.

For a couple of hours
we don't speak.

But our eyes meet
again and again.

Until we're sitting
on the same couch.

Making
small talk.

While everyone else is
making out.

The room empties
around us.

Kate is with Eric,
somewhere.

Abby left,
with someone.

But Morgan and I
stay up for hours
talking.

The sky outside
is getting lighter.

It's morning
when we
kiss.

Top of the list,
no contest...

Best.
Kiss.
Ever.

WHAT I KNOW ABOUT THIS GUY SO FAR

We love most of the same books.
(A guy who reads!)

A lot of the same bands.
(A must.)

Some of the same movies.
(A plus.)

He's really into football.
(I can look past this.)

He knows how to make me laugh.
(He's *really* funny.)

I can tell from the start
he's just not like these
other guys.

He's got
style.

And
class.

(And, most importantly,
he's single.)

BLUR

I'm eye level
with his teeth.

These two perfect rows
of pearly whites.

Which he's always
showcasing,
smiling.

Which he's ruining
with cigarettes.

But still.

(He's trying
to quit.)

I can't decide
what color his eyes are.

(Perhaps hazel.)

Behind glasses,
most days.

(Unless he's
wearing contacts.)

Brown hair,
a little messy.

(Sometimes he wears
a hat.)

I try on his hat.

And we trade
glasses.

His lenses
are much stronger
than mine.

And
everything
is a
b l u r.

THE CATCH

There's just one
teeny
tiny
itsy
bitsy
little
really
very
small
problem.

He's 19.

And I'm still 16.

But going on 17!

I told him I'm 18.

A tiny
not-truth.

All I know is,
my parents
won't be
meeting Morgan
any time
soon.

IN SCHOOL

Too distracted
to focus
or care.

I wonder what Morgan
is up to
right now.

He's in
     college.

He has his own
     apartment.

Suddenly my life feels
so lame.

Gym (or study hall),
chemistry,
history,
lunch,
trig,
media studies,
psych,
and
English.

Then home to my
parents' house.

And my bedroom
still painted pink
from when I was a kid.

All I can do now
is look forward to
the weekend.

SENIORITIS

I think I have senioritis,
Kate says.

I'm only
half listening.

She always thinks
she has something.
The flu. Or the plague.

What is that?
Abby asks.

Senioritis?
Kate asks.

Yeah!
Abby and I say together.

You know!
Kate explains.

*It's when seniors slack off
during their last year
of high school!*

But we're only JUNIORS!
Abby laughs.

I think I have senioritis, too,
I admit.

We're BAD,
Kate laughs.

Abby smiles and says,
*I knew you'd come around
someday!*

DROWNING

I'm at the bottom of the ocean
holding my breath.

I don't want to swim
to the surface yet.

It's so pretty
down here.

Colorful creatures
and plants I've
never seen before.

When I realize
that I can't wait
any longer,
I
kick
toward
the
surface
but
it's
too
late.

I've
been
under
water
far
too
long
and
the
sky
is
too
far
away.

I wake up
              gasping
for air.

STUFF

Morgan and Eric's place
is just kind of
the party house now.

We hang out there
pretty much
every weekend.

Sometimes weeknights,
which are a little harder
to get away with.

We usually
spend the night.

Kate and Eric
are hooking up
I guess.

Even though she's
still dating
Trevor.

Even though Eric
has a girlfriend
out of town.

But I mind
my own
business.

I'm too busy
hanging out with
Morgan.

When the party
dies down
we stay up late.

Lying in bed,
listening to records.

And making out,
and stuff.

NONE OF YOUR BUSINESS

One morning
I overhear Eric
grilling Morgan
in the kitchen.

*So what's up
with you and Paige?*

He wants to know.

*Are you guys
doing it
or something?*

He wants to know.

Morgan just laughs.

*That's none of
your business,*
he says.

*You know I don't
kiss and tell.*

JUNIOR PROM

is still a long
way off.

But I can't help
thinking about it.

I mean,
it's probably
going to be
kind of lame.

The school dances
always are.

But I never
miss one.

I'm only going to be
a teenager
once.

But.

I can't take
Morgan.

For one thing,
he thinks I'm
a senior.

Even if I was,
I doubt he'd
want to go to
a high school dance.

And another thing,
I feel like
I really
probably
can't let
anybody
know
about this
relationship.

My parents
would certainly
            try
to put
an end to it.

They'd probably
never let me
leave the house
again.

I'm glad
junior prom
is still a long
way off.

A MONDAY, NOVEMBER

Mr. Bates stands
at the front of the room.
Arms crossed,
but smiling.

Waiting for the students
to file in
one by one,
unsmiling.

Class!
He exclaims.
Before today's lesson—
a quick announcement!
Ms. Smith and I are
starting that writing club
that I told you about!

It's Tuesdays
after school
in this room.

I write down the details
even though
I'm not interested anymore.

I hope to see some of you there!

He smiles
and looks right at me.

MONDAY NIGHT

I should be
doing homework
right now.

I have
so much of it.

But I can't
focus.

Because Morgan
is out with his friends.

At a bar.

They all have
fake IDs.

And I'm stuck here.
Feeling left
                out.

What if he's
meeting
other girls?

It's not that
I don't
trust him.

It's just that
I don't trust
the alcohol.

I try listening
to music.

But even my
favorite songs
can't cheer me up
tonight.

SOS

Morgan agrees
to pick me up.

So I wait for
Mom and Dad
to go to bed.

Then I sneak
                out.

Morgan
and his friend Tim
are parked at the corner.

We head back
to Tim's place.

It's nice being out
without Kate and Abby
for a change.

I drink
while the guys smoke.

We watch weird,
funny movies.

And talk about everything
and nothing.

Tim pours me another drink
saying,

We've been out all night.
You have some catching up to do.

I'm a lightweight.

But I want to prove
that I'm not a lightweight.

A few drinks later
Morgan takes my glass away.

Okay, I think you've
had enough,
he says.

But he laughs
and kisses me anyway.

WHAT WAS I THINKING?

Morgan drives
me home,
dropping me off
at the bottom
of the driveway.

The sun
is almost
up.

But no one
is awake
yet.

And I sneak
into the house
without making
too much noise.

I'm lucky
I don't
get caught.

Because I know
I would be
grounded
for the rest
of my
life.

TUESDAY

I didn't sleep
at all last night
and in the morning
it shows.

For gym class
we have
a fitness test.

We're supposed to do
100 crunches.

Kate and I
take turns
holding each other's
feet.

Kate does
all 100.

I do six
and excuse myself
to vomit
in the bathroom.

*Did you go out
last night?*
Kate asks.

I know
she'll be mad
that I didn't
invite her.

No,

I lie.

*I think
I'm just
coming down
with something.*

THE END OF A LONG DAY

*Will you be coming back
for writing club?*

asks Mr. Bates.

I'm collecting my books
and getting up to leave.

Yeah, maybe!

I lie,
cheerfully.

As if I don't have
better things
to do.

THE NIGHT IS YOUNG

Kate parallel parks
and makes it
on the third try.

Abby digs through her purse
for a cigarette
and lighter.

I chomp a piece of gum
and pass the pack around
to share.

Abby runs a brush
through her hair
for the hundredth time.

Kate checks her makeup
in the overhead
mirror.

Finally, we're ready
for another
party.

SMOKE CIRCLE

We lean on
damp furniture
on the front porch
passing a blunt.

I take a drag
though I can't
seem to do it right.

Not sure
if I can't.

Or if
I won't.

The thought of
my lungs
blackening
stops me mid-breath.

Smoke burns my throat
and I cough.

Amateur...
Abby laughs.

It's passed around
a couple more times
and comes back
wet and soggy.

I try to inhale
once more
but my heart just
isn't in it.

I'm not sure
if I feel the weed
or if I'm just
drunk.

I'm glad
when it's down
to nothing.

And Tim crumbles it
between his fingers
and tosses it
into the snow.

DO I COUNT THIS ONE?

I go to the kitchen
for a drink.

Eric is digging
for a beer
in the glow
of the fridge
and hands
me one,
too.

We lean on the counter
and chat.

He's asks,
So what's up with you and Morgan?

And I tease,
None of your business...
You know I don't kiss and tell...

Oh, really? Eric
grabs my face.

He kisses me on the mouth
with force.

So hard
it actually
hurts.

I hear somebody walk in
and turn around saying,
Heyyyy...sorry!

I turn my face, and push Eric away,
though he's already
letting go.

What the heck?!
Dude, that is so
not cool!

I want to scream at him
but instead I just
stammer.

Sorry, he says.
You know I'm
just messing with you!

He laughs
and walks away.

ROUGH SEAS

I wonder who saw us
and what they're thinking.

And who they told,
if anyone.

Maybe it's best
to say nothing.

But a couple of beers later
I decide to talk
to Morgan.

I find him
surrounded by friends.

Right away, it seems like
he's angry.

Did somebody tell him
something?

I say,
Hey, we need to talk.
But he storms off.

I text him,
Hey, we need to talk.
No response.

I'll give him some space,
wait for things to
calm down.

But then,
not 15 minutes later,
Morgan is sitting on the couch
with some girl
on his lap.

They're laughing
and whispering.

He touches
her hair.

I'm too embarrassed
to step in.

I'm not going
to cause a scene.

A few guys I know
shoot me nervous glances.

One of them
puts their hand
on my shoulder.

What's going on?
they want to know.

Is everything all right?

But I can't
speak.

Through my tears,
everything is a
b l u r.

Like I'm wearing
Morgan's glasses.

IT'S OVER.

When

I

see

them

KISS

my

HE   ART

breaks

in

two.

END SCENE

One by one
everyone leaves.

Most of them stumble down
the front stairs.

One climbs out of
a window.

Morgan and the new girl
disappear into his room.

And I'm alone
in the living room.

Kate and I had planned on
spending the night here.

I don't want to tell her
what happened.

And I haven't seen her
in a while.

Probably in Eric's room
by now.

Probably too drunk to drive
anyway.

I guess I could call a
taxi.

It doesn't feel safe to go
alone.

At this hour.

And I can't show up at my house
now.

It's 3 a.m.

I'm supposed to be at a
sleepover.

So I lie down on the
couch.

In the dark,
I stare at the ceiling.

I realize the front door
is still wide   open.

And there are no bodies left
to warm the room.

But I can't be bothered
to move.

A LONG NIGHT

I'm on
his couch.

The only thing separating me and them is his bedroom wall.

She's in
his bed.

FALLING

I
fell
for him.

It just
felt
right.

But things
fell
undone.

In one
fell
swoop.

I guess I just
fell
out of favor.

I won't be
falling
asleep tonight.

IN THE MORNING LIGHT

Finger-tip shaped
bruises
on my jaw.

A fat lip
and a
broken heart.

Kate only notices
my puffy
red eyes.

She waits
until we're in the car
to ask.

What happened?

I'm already
pretending
it's nothing.

We broke up.
It's okay.
I'm over it.

I knew it wouldn't last
anyway.

Didn't I?

ENGLISH CLASS

Sitting in last period
again.

I fake it through
the entire class.
No one realizes
I didn't do the reading.

Then the bell rings—finally
freedom.

Mr. Bates speaks
just loud enough
for me to hear
over the shuffle of papers.

Paige,
can you stay a minute,
please?

Everybody turns to glance at me.
Wondering what I've done.

Staying after class
is for troublemakers
and nerds.

Which one am I?

BUSTED

He must know
I didn't read
the book.

Mr. Bates shuffles papers
on his desk for a minute
saying nothing,
while the room empties.

The last students
disappear through
the doorway.

Mr. Bates sits
on the edge of his desk.
Trying to look casual.

Is everything okay?

he asks.

Yeah, of course.

What else am I supposed to say?

*If there's anything troubling you,
you can talk to me
or any of your teachers.
Any time.*

Okay...

I say with a straight face.

Have a nice day, Paige.

Thank you, Mr. Bates.

And I leave this moment
in the dust.

REBOUND

Forget all the drama.
I just want to have fun.

There are so many
other guys out there.

We go to Eric's party
on Friday.
I'm glad that
Morgan is at work.

Abby and Kate
are my allies
at war with
Morgan.

Alcohol
is our
ammo.

I drink more than usual
to prove that I don't care.

(But instead it shows
that I care a lot.)

I spend the night
flirting
with a guy
I've never met.

His name is
Bobby.

Nothing really
happened,
but we fell asleep
on the couch together.

When I wake up
in the morning
I feel
ill.

But I realize that Morgan
had to walk past us
when he got home
last night.

And secretly,
I'm glad.

SNOW BALL

I almost forgot
about the Snow Ball.
It's our school's
winter dance.

Kate is going with Trevor.

She laughs,
We can't let our parents know
who we really hang out with.

Abby found a date,
some guy named Shawn.

I was starting to get nervous
I wouldn't find anyone.

But then
Alex Parish asked me!

   Mixed emotions.

I always liked him.
(Really, really liked him.
Since forever.)
And I guess...I still do?

   But he doesn't drink.
   How will this be
   any fun?

THE NIGHT OF THE DANCE

Kate and I meet
at my house
to do our hair
and makeup.

We borrow old dresses
from each other.

Because we'd rather
save our money
for alcohol.

Our dates show up
with a few other friends.

Alex gives me a
flower to wear
on my wrist.

Our moms take pictures
in the living room.

We all smile and say,
Cheese!

SHAWN

I don't know how Abby's date
is allowed at the school dance.

They show up drunk
and high.

He has tattoos
that are so old
they're already fading.

And he shaves his head
to hide that he's balding.

But no one at school
seems to notice.

They leave early
without saying
goodbye.

HAVING A BALL?

It's the same old
high school dance.

Everybody mingles
and moves around
more awkwardly
than we'd like to admit.

Alex is a good dancer.

I am not.

We agree that the music
is not our usual taste.

But when a slow song comes on
he puts his arms around me
and it just feels
right.

I'm a little
surprised.

I'm having more fun
with this kid
than I thought I would.

BURGER BUDDIES

The dance is over
before anyone feels ready
to go home.

So we decide to go
for something to eat
at the late-night diner
down the street.

Alex and I
both order
veggie burgers
with fries.

Aw, you're burger buddies!
A match made in heaven!
Kate laughs.

And I elbow her
in the ribs.
A little harder
than I should.

XO, OR NO?

I'm sad
when it's time
to say goodnight.

But I'm still thinking
of someone
else.

HE TEXTED ME

Morgan must have
seen all the photos
we posted from
the Snow Ball.

I know he's just trying
to have the final word.

But he texted me.

I want to see you.

I know he's just trying
to prove that I still want him.

But isn't that the truth?

He wants to see me!

I'm trying
to play it cool.

But I am so
not playing it cool.

OUR ANNUAL SHOPPING TRIP

I go shopping
with Kate and Abby
at the mall.

The holidays
are approaching.

We're looking for gifts
for our families.

And searching the sales racks
for ourselves.

I buy a sweater
for Mom.

A book
for Dad.

And some weird toy
Logan wants.

We take a break
from shopping.

And get hot pretzels
and lemonade
in the food court.

Kate and Abby
are talking
about the next party.

But my mind is somewhere else.
Wondering if I should get
a gift for Morgan.

I don't want him
to know I care
more than he does.

HOLIDAY CHEER

Last day of school
before break!
Then
freedom!

Everybody is wearing
their favorite
ugly holiday sweaters
and Santa hats.

By the end of the day
I can't believe
we barely have
any homework.

Kate and I
are making faces
at each other
from across the room.

The whole class
is a little wound up.
Maybe we're too old
to be acting so silly.

But nobody can seem
to contain their excitement.
Even our teachers are in
an extra jolly mood today.

A MAJOR ASSIGNMENT

Only a minute left
in the day.

We all start to pack up
our books and papers.

I almost forgot!
Your assignment this break...
starts Mr. Bates.

Everyone moans.

What? You said we
didn't have any homework!
A few people mumble.

Your assignment this break...
repeats Mr. Bates,
is to have fun!

And be SAFE!
he adds.

Kate and I
shoot each other a look
and laugh.

We all charge out
through the door
the second the bell rings.

WINTER BREAK

I could stay in and bake cookies
with mom.

Or play video games
with Logan.

Why don't you two build a snowman?
Mom asks.
Or go sledding down at the park?

Yeah right!

All I want to do
is party
with my friends.

Going out for hot chocolate
with Kate!
I lie.

Mom's shouts,
Be careful out there!
or something.

But I can hardly hear
as the screen door
slams behind me.

Can't wait to see
Morgan.

OCEANS APART

We've never talked about
what happened that night.

I just wish everything could be
normal between us
again.

But was it
ever?

I always think that
the next time I see him
I'll have the words
and the guts
to say everything
I need to say.

But the words
don't come.

WAVES

Maybe   a
     after

few   drinks
     more

but   again
     then

I   want
     don't

to   waves
     make

DRINKING GAMES

Sometimes
we play
drinking
games.

As if
we don't
drink
enough
without
games.

Sometimes
we play
to drink.

And sometimes
we drink
to play.

It's a bit
foolish
either
way.

TRUTH OR DARE?

Dare:
Eric makes a snow angel
in his underwear.

Dare:
Kate kisses Abby
on the lips.

Dare:
Morgan chugs
another beer.

Dare:
Abby runs down the street
topless.

Truth:
I have never ever
shoplifted.

Truth:
Eric has tried
every drug we can name.

Dare:
Eric tells Kate to kiss Morgan,
but Morgan refuses.

Truth:
I am relieved.

WORLDS APART

I say,
Hey,
we need to talk.

> Morgan says,
> *What's up?*

Remember
that night?

> *What night?*

Did somebody tell you
that Eric kissed me?

> *Ha ha, no.*
> *What are you talking about?*

Oh.
He kissed me.
One night.
But I didn't want him to...

> *Well, it's not a big deal.*
> *You can kiss*
> *whoever.*
> *It's not like we've*
> *ever been*
> *that serious.*

I know,
I lie.

And I don't know
what is real
anymore.

THIS OR NOTHING

We're
not really
going out.

But at least
we're
hanging out.

And stuff.

I'll take this
over
nothing.

For now.

WHO ELSE HAS HE BEEN WITH?

The more
I drink
about it
the less
I think
about it.

STAYING AFLOAT

I'm floating on a raft
in the middle of the ocean.

The sky is clear and
the sun is bright.

But a dark cloud
moves in.

The water grows
choppy.

Kate and Abby
are nearby,
struggling.

I call to them
and reach out.

But I, too,
am sinking.

My raft has turned into
a giant glass bottle.

I lose my grip
and fall off.

The waves feel
sticky.

We start to drink.

Because maybe
if we drink enough,
the ocean will dry up
and our feet will reach
the earth below.

We drink
and drink
and drink.

We're so close.

But I get
woozy.

And just as I feel
my feet settle
onto the soft
ocean floor,
I tip into the
shallow sea
facedown
and pass out.

When I wake up
I'm lying on my
bedroom floor.

Haven't fallen
out of bed
since I was
too young
to remember.

PROCRASTINATORS

It's Sunday night.
The last night
of winter break.

We have to go to school
in the morning.

      But first,
      one more party.

Kate and I tell our parents,
*We're having a sleepover at Abby's
again.*

We have to finish a project,
we lie.

We put it off until the last minute,
we lie.

      It's poetry.

Which is only
               sort of
                         a lie.

Mom is not surprised.
I'm a good student,
but even she knows,
a procrastinator.

I don't know about this,
Mom says.

A sleepover on a school night?

She is not too happy about it.

Make sure you aren't late for school
in the morning!
She warns.
Or else this will be
the LAST sleepover
you ever have!

We can't be late!
I tell Kate
when I get in her car.

Agreed!

Kate says.

My mom said
the exact same thing!

IN DISGUISE

We're going to a party
but I look like I'm going
to a sleepover.

I leave home wearing an old sweatshirt
but I change into my favorite top
and put on makeup
in the car.

I take down two long braids
so that my hair falls
in waves.

And ditch my glasses
even though I
don't own
contacts.

Now everyone can see my eyes
even if I can't see theirs.

It's not supposed
to be a big deal.

Just a few people
hanging out.

But one of them
happens to be
Morgan.

THE HANGOUT

It's a good night.
An amazing, drama-free night.

We hang out in the living room
playing cards.

Drinking games
that have everyone laughing.

And arguing—
though it's all in good fun.

Morgan has his arm around me
the whole time.

Even Eric is acting sweet
and fun to be around.

Kate plays the role of DJ
and changes every song halfway through.

Abby and Tim
seem to be hitting it off.

I behave myself
for the most part.

I mean
compared to the usual.

So maybe I did drink
a little too much.

Nobody pays attention
to the time.

Until we all go to bed
at around 5 a.m.

*We can't be late
for school tomorrow!*

Kate and I agree
and shake on it.

*I think you mean
that you can't be late
today!*

laughs Morgan.

He's right.

I can hardly believe
we have to leave for school
in a couple of hours.

RISE AND SHINE

It feels like I just closed my eyes.

But Kate is already pounding
on Morgan's bedroom door.

I look at my phone.
It's 8:00 a.m.

Come on! Hurry up!
Kate yells.

*The bell for first period
is going to ring in five minutes!*

And we're 20 minutes away.

Fifteen if we make
good time.

I'm so tired
and already can't wait
for the day to be over.

Kate waits in the car
while I brush my teeth,
splash water on my face,
and run a comb through my hair.

Kate honks the car horn.

Even Abby is ready to go,
sitting in the passenger seat.

I feel dizzy.

I pull open the door,
and climb in the back.

The sun reflects
off the snow and cars.

Too bright,
blazing through
the windows.

Head pounding.
Ears ringing.

I am
        spinning.

And mad at myself
for doing this to myself
again.

Next time
I won't go
            overboard.

CAPTAIN KATE

Are you okay to drive?
I ask Kate, out of habit.

Yeah, I feel fine,
she says.

She turns the key.
The radio is blasting
turned up too high
from the night before.

The car lurches forward.
Hubcaps scrape the curb
a little bit.

She makes a quick
three-point turn
and takes off
down the street.

I bet I can catch
a quick nap.

I stretch out in the back seat
using my backpack as a pillow.

I put an arm over my eyes
and drift off.

! ! !

I wake to the sound
                    of tires screeching
                                        and glass
breaking.

!   !
    !   !
        !   !
            !   !
                    !
            !   !
                !   !
        !   !
    !   !
!   !

I am spinning.
                I am spinning.
                                I am spinning.

And then what
                I remember
                                is nothing.
Because for the
                first time ever
                                I black out.

OUT

I must be asleep.
Or something.

Time passes
quickly
but I move
s l o w l y.

I wander the halls
of a strange apartment
looking for Morgan.

There is a locked door
that I think he is behind.

I hear laughter and whispers
and I'm afraid to knock.

Further down the hall
I find Abby and Kate
soaking in a bathtub
full of ice.

Abby says,
Come in!

Kate says,
We lost the war.

WHEN I COME TO

Bright lights above.

Eyes swollen.

Head in bandages.

One arm in a cast.

Too hot?

Or too cold?

I feel everything.

I feel nothing.

Kate? Abby?

Mom says,
They're okay, honey.

Dad says,
Just rest.

WHAT HAPPENED?

I remember very little.
But am filled in
on the details.

Kate ran a red light.
Causing another car
to hit us.

Abby broke her arm.
Kate broke her nose.
And lost her license.

She won't be able to drive again
for a long,
long time.

And we all have to do
community service.

But it's a small
price to pay.

I'm the only one who was
seriously injured.

I don't need anybody to tell me
how lucky we are
that nobody
got killed.

But they
tell me
anyway…

You're a lucky lady.

At least you were wearing a seat belt.

Lucky to be alive.

Could have killed somebody.

You're smarter than this.

I hope you learned something from this.

Thank god nobody died.

You could have died.

UNSPOKEN

Mom is more upset
than angry.
She doesn't talk about
what happened.

Beyond her silence
I hear the questions
she'll never ask.

What was she thinking?
How did I not see this coming?
She's a good kid.
They're all good kids.
Straight As.
She doesn't drink.
Does she?
Were they doing drugs?
They couldn't be.
Where could they even find drugs?
Or alcohol, for that matter?
Where were they all night?
Who were they with?
Boys?
Men?

She will never ask,
but she will
always wonder.

THE THOUGHT THAT COUNTS

All of my
teachers
send cards
signed by
all of my
classmates.

> *Get well soon!*

>   *Thinking of you!*

> *Speedy recovery!*

>   *In our prayers!*

Some of my family
and closest friends
send flowers.

I wait for
a text
or a call
from Morgan.

Radio silence.

MY JOURNAL

Mom brings
my journal
from home.

In case you want to write,
she says.

But I tell her,
I don't want to.

OUTSIDE MY WINDOW

The sun goes

      up
        and
          down

      up
        and
          down

      up
        and
          down.

As the world *spins*

         around

   and   and

 around   around

   and   and

        around

A VISITOR

I'm sorry,
Kate says.
I'm so sorry.

I know,
I say.
I know.

Kate is grounded
for the rest of the year.

And so am I
once I get out of here.

It's nothing
in light of everything.

How's Abby?
I ask.

I haven't seen her.
She stopped coming to school.
Doesn't answer my texts...
I'm sorry.

I know.

We talk about
other things
instead.

THE DRIVE HOME

When it's time to leave the hospital
I'm afraid to get
in the car.

Dad drives and
Mom sits
up front.

I grip the door handle
waiting to
crash.

My stomach lurches
with every stop
and go.

The world outside
the window
is fast
and loud.

Inside the car
nobody
makes
a sound.

HOME

Back in my own
familiar
pink room.

With my own
soft bedsheets
and blankets.

Far from
the harsh buzz
of hospital sounds.

No beeping machines.
No crying strangers.
No shuffling feet.

But there are still
hushed voices
from Mom and Dad
in the rooms below.

Even Logan
keeps quiet,
shuffling around
is his socks.

Spying on me
from the hallway.
Curious but
keeping his distance.

RUIN

I spend whole days
just lying in bed.

Thinking.

And crying.

I feel sick.
I feel like a fool.

My family,
my teachers,
my friends,
and classmates
and even their parents—
I don't want to see
any of them
now.

How will I
show my face
in public
ever again?

How can I
go back
to school?

THE FUNERAL

In the dark
at night
with my eyes
closed,
I *spin*.

When I sit up
I can see
from the window
of a car.

Three long holes
in the earth.

My family
in tears.

Everyone I know
dressed in black.

Three dark caskets
balanced on ropes
going down
       and
          down
            and
               down
                 and
                   down.

THE TRUTH

Mom stands in the doorway
of my bedroom.

How do you feel?
Are you okay?

she asks me
for the millionth time.

She's careful.

Afraid to stir me
from this silence
that is the only opposite
of crying.

No,

I admit.

Because
I am so sick
of telling
lies.

A SPARK

The next morning
I wake up feeling rested
for the first time
in months.

Sharper.

Things come into
focus.

I reach for my journal
and a pen.

And I write.

Mom checks in on me.
Sees me with my nose
in my notebook.

And returns a little later
with chocolate chip pancakes.

I write all day,
getting up a few times
to do chores.

Vacuuming the stairs.

Helping with dinner.

But afterwards
I write some more.

And when I finally
look up from my journal
the sky outside
is dark.

Mom stands in my
open doorway
but knocks
anyway.

Don't stay up too late.
You need your rest.

Still she smiles
seeing me work.

DOUBTS

I hear a voice inside
telling me,

*You have nothing
important
to say.*

But I hear another voice
telling me,

*Keep writing
anyway.*

BOOKWORM

I have to miss a
couple more weeks of class
to stay home and rest.
Doctor's orders.

But my schoolwork
is sent home.

I spend hours
staring blankly at math
and chemistry worksheets.

Unable to focus.

Unwilling to focus.

But I catch up
on all the reading
for history and English class.

I'd forgotten how much
I love to read.

By the end of the second week
I'm feeling bored and restless.

I think I'm finally ready
to get back to my classes.

BACK TO SCHOOL

Dad drops me off
in front of school.

The walk to my locker
through the crowded halls
feels like it takes
forever.

Everything looks
different.

The ceilings are lower.
The hallways are longer.

Was it always
this loud?

By the time I get there
I find that I cannot remember
my locker combination.

The secretary in the office
is confused by my request.

But the school year's halfway through,
she says, shaking her head.

BEST FRIENDS

I'm excused from gym class
for a few weeks.
Until my cast comes off
and everything.

So I don't see Kate
until lunch.

I find her at our
usual table.
Picking at her salad
with a fork.

We wonder where Abby is.
As always.

Then we sit
in silence.
Unsure of what
to talk about.

But sometimes
that's okay.

WARM WELCOME

The day feels so much
l   o   n   g   e   r.

By last period
I'm dead tired.

Mr. Bates smiles
when he sees me.

Welcome back, Paige!

From the class,
a few nods,
and a wave.

Mostly just
blank stares
and whispers.

Kate blushes
and puts her face
in a book.

Mr. Bates dives
right into the lesson,
and I'm thankful.

OLD ME OR NEW ME?

Writing Club members!
Don't forget to bring
a piece to share
tomorrow!

Mr. Bates
reminds the class
as we file out.

Maybe we'll see you there, Paige?

Yeah,
I mumble.
Maybe.

But as I cross the room
I feel sure of it.

Yes,
I say.
Definitely.

A little
surprised
with myself.

Because this time
I'm not even
lying.

WORD SEARCH

I stay up late
flipping through my journal.

Trying to choose
a piece of writing to share.

It's hard to pick just one
after all I've written
this month.

I type it up neatly
on my computer
and print it out.

I read it over
again
and
again.

Am I really
doing this?

I read it
again.
And
again
and
again
and
again.

RESTLESS

Can't

      seem

to

      fall

            asleep

      tonight.

My

      mind

is

      everywhere.

SWEET DREAMS

My right hand is glowing.

    With a flick of my wrist,

        I write words in gold,

            strung across the sky

                loopy letters in the clouds,

                    beautiful sparkling ribbons.

                I'm delighted with myself.

            Until
                the words
            start
              to

c   r   u   m   b   l   e

        and

b   r   e   a   k
                a   p   a   r t.

                    Pieces shower down like

                      the ashes of fireworks.

ANOTHER TUESDAY

I can't wait
for this school day
to be over!

But for once
I'm not
complaining.

I'm just
really excited
for writing club today!

(And a little nervous,
too.)

@PAIGETHEPOET

Hey, Paige!

Oh no.

It's Alex.

Coming toward
my locker.

I've been avoiding him
since the accident.

Because I know
he probably
hates me now.

How are you feeling?
he asks.

I'm doing okay...
Thanks for the card!

I'd almost forgotten
that he sent me one
at the hospital.

What are you
up to today?
Alex asks.

I've got writing club
after school,
I tell him.

That's awesome.
I didn't know you were a writer!
Alex says.

Yeah,
I say.
Mostly a poet,
I add.

Paige the Poet,
he says.
And my burger buddy.

And I actually
laugh
out loud.

I'm going to have to
yell at Kate later,
for starting
that terrible
nickname.

Though I have to admit
I don't mind it as much
coming from Alex.

LAST PERIOD ENDS

Kate winks and
gives me a
thumbs-up.

Good luck!
she whispers.

Stay!
I plead.

But she's already
running out
the door.

WHAT AM I DOING HERE?

This was a really
bad idea.

What was I even
thinking?

My poem probably
stinks.

Maybe I should just
go home.

I'm about to get up
to leave.

But Mr. Bates
chimes in,

*Paige! I'm so glad
you decided
to stay!*

IN TOO DEEP

We have a new member!
announces Mr. Bates.
Paige is joining us today!

The club is in full swing.
There's no escaping now.

A few familiar faces.
And a few unfamiliar.

I'm not sure which ones
I'm more nervous about.

Ms. Smith talks next,
but I'm too distracted
to listen.

Then, one at a time
students start taking turns
reading out loud
a short story
or a poem.

Some of them seem
even more nervous
than I am!

DEEP BREATHS

I'm really impressed
with the amount of talent
in this room.

And a little scared,
too.

When it's my turn to read,
my hands shake.

I stare at my paper
even though I have it memorized.

Mr. Bates crosses his arms
and nods his head
while he listens.

This is powerful stuff.
Powerful stuff,
he says
when I'm done.

He says this
to everyone.

(But I think
only because
it's true.)

ONE TOO MANY LIES
by Paige Miller

All of the fibs
and little white lies.
Like a flurry of snowflakes
in front of our eyes.

We lied to each other,
our family, and friends.
We took it too far
...all the way to the end.

The more that we told them
the thicker they grew.
Until there was a blizzard
clouding our view.

Even lied to myself
and I know you have, too.
We spun works of fiction
until nothing was true.

Lies blind like sunbeams.
They cut like a knife.
So take care with your words.
They could mean your life.

WANT TO KEEP READING?

If you liked this book, check out another book

from West 44 Books:

WHAT IF BY ANNA RUSSELL

ISBN: 9781538382578

OFFBEAT: PART ONE

My thoughts don't bother me

        here.

Drumsticks resting
between middle-finger
knuckle and my thumb.
Pointer finger

     r e l a x e d

against the wood. I hit
the snare.

       tap
       taptaptap
       tap
       taptap

Marching band beats.

When I'm drumming, things feel

        right.

Like finally fitting a puzzle piece
into its spot.

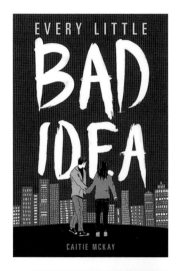

ABOUT THE AUTHOR

L. A. Bowen is a writer and artist, among other things. In addition to creating works of fiction, she designs children's books, plays in a rock band, and raises ostriches. One of these things is a lie. Bowen's stories are inspired by the adventures and misadventures of her teenage years. She lives with her husband and three cats in Buffalo, New York. Check out more at labowen.com.